T0166704

My Very First Look at
Words

CHANHASSEN, MINNESOTA • LONDON

www.two-canpublishing.com

Published in the United States and Canada by Two-Can Publishing
18705 Lake Drive East, Chanhassen, MN 55317

© Two-Can Publishing 2003

Conceived, designed and edited by

Picthall & Gunzi Ltd

21A Widmore Road, Bromley, Kent BR1 1RW

Original concept: Chez Picthall
Editor: Margaret Hynes
Designer: Paul Calver
Photography: Steve Gorton
Additional photographs: Daniel Pangbourne
DTP: Tony Cutting, Ray Bryant

All rights reserved. No part of this publication may be reproduced, stored in
a retrieval system, or transmitted in any form or by any means electronic,
mechanical, photocopying, recording or otherwise, without
prior written permission of the publisher.

'Two-Can' is a trademark of Two-Can Publishing.
Two-Can Publishing is a division of Creative Publishing international, Inc.
18705 Lake Drive East, Chanhassen MN 55317
1-800-328-3895
www.two-canpublishing.com

ISBN 1–58728–670–X (HC)
ISBN 1-58728-684-X (SC)
ISBN 1-58728-589-4 (ALB)

2 4 6 8 10 9 7 5 3 1

Color reproduction by Reed Digital.
Printed in Hong Kong.

key: b = bottom, c = centre, l = left, r = right, t = top):

The publisher would like to thank the following people, companies and organizations
for their kind permission to reproduce their photographs:

Multiyork: 6tr, 7bc; Sony UK: 7br

My Very First Look at
Words

Christiane Gunzi

CHANHASSEN, MINNESOTA • LONDON

Clothes

gloves

sweater

hat

skirt

socks

sneakers

Can you find the sweater?

jacket

dress

shoes

shirt

T-shirt

pants

What color are the shoes?

In my home

clock

lamp

chair

newspaper

frying pan

What helps you to tell the time?

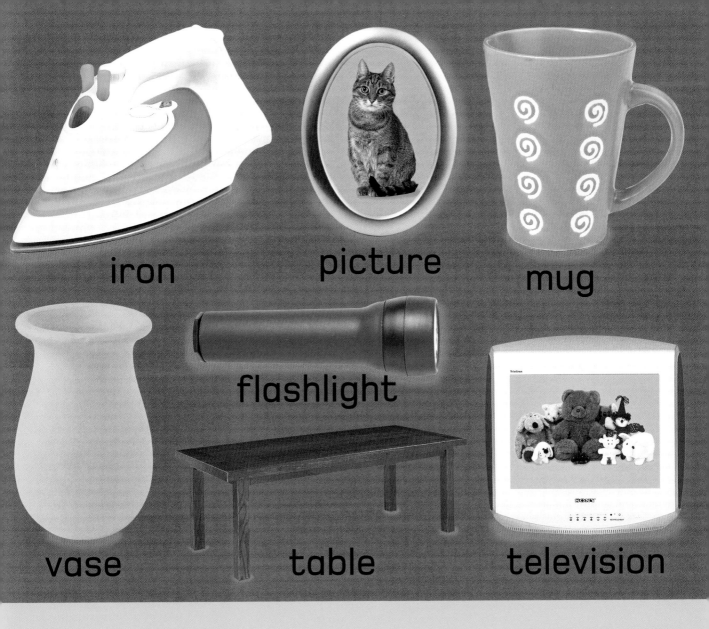

iron

picture

mug

flashlight

vase

table

television

Point to the blue things!

Food and drink

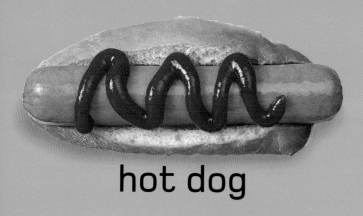

hot dog

toasted cheese

pasta

orange juice

pizza

What shape is the slice of pizza?

french fries

apple

cake

eggs

hamburger

milk

grapes

Which drink do you like best?

Toys

car

yo-yo

sailing boat

teddy bear

drum

robot

Which toy floats on water?

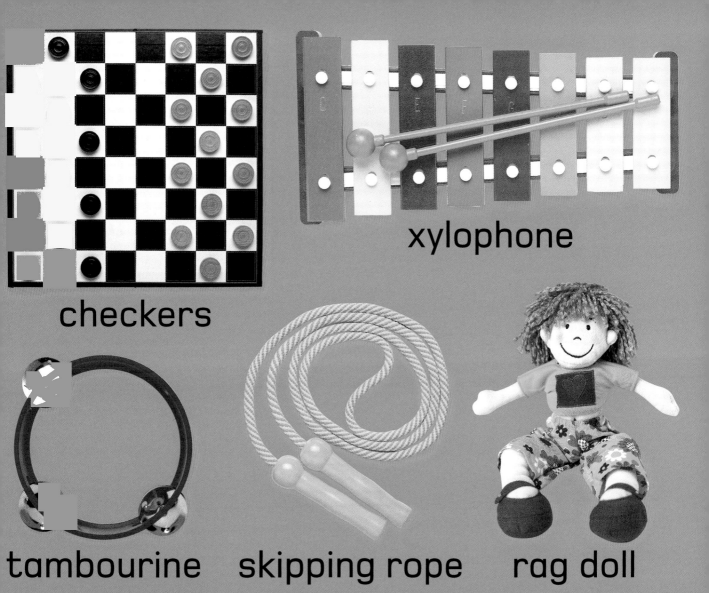

checkers

xylophone

tambourine skipping rope rag doll

Point to the musical instruments!

School things

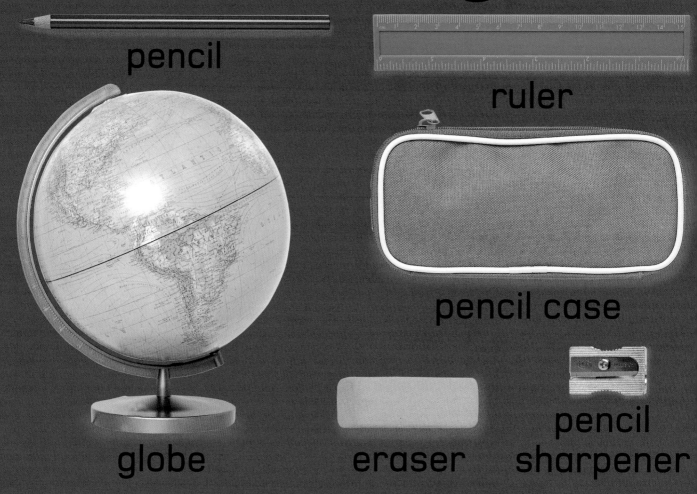

pencil

ruler

pencil case

globe

eraser

pencil sharpener

Where do you keep your pencils?

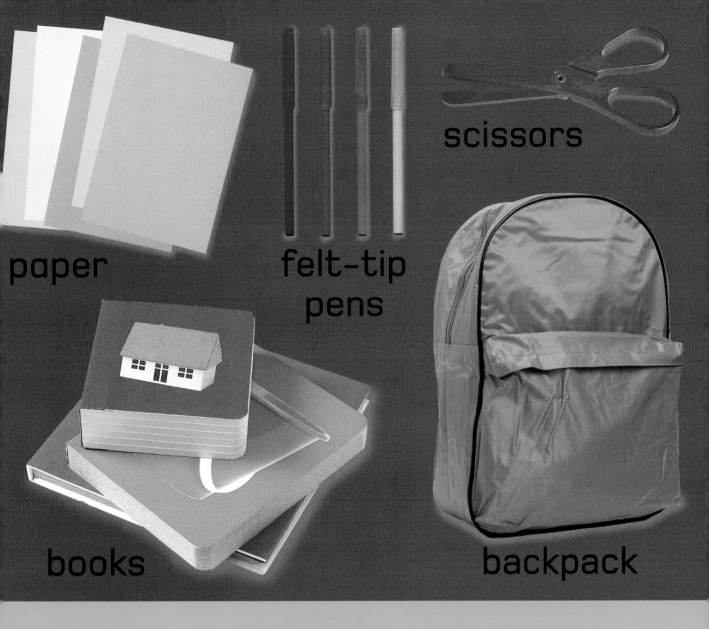

paper

felt-tip pens

scissors

books

backpack

Count the felt-tip pens!

Things that go

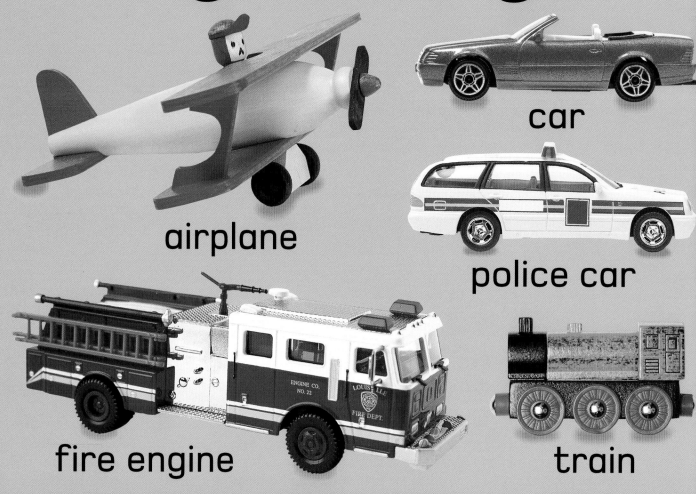

airplane

car

police car

fire engine

train

Point to the things that fly!

ambulance

tractor

helicopter

truck

Which of these is the longest?

Animals

alligator

cow

fish

frog

horse

tiger

Point to the striped animals!

snake

sheep

elephant

zebra

hippopotamus

giraffe

Which animal is the tallest?

Colors

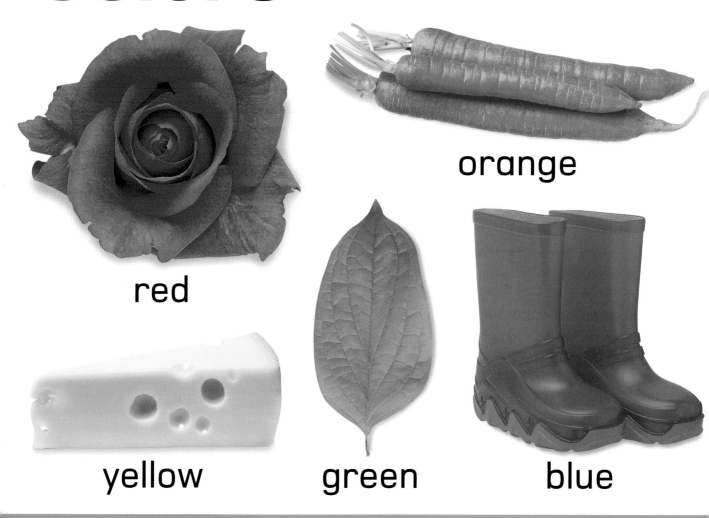

orange

red

yellow   green   blue

What color is the flower?

pink

purple

brown

gray

gold

silver

black

white

What shape are the gold coins?

Shapes

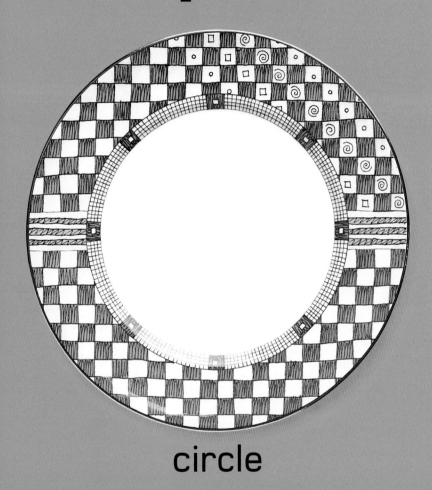

circle

triangle

square

Can you find the teddy bear?

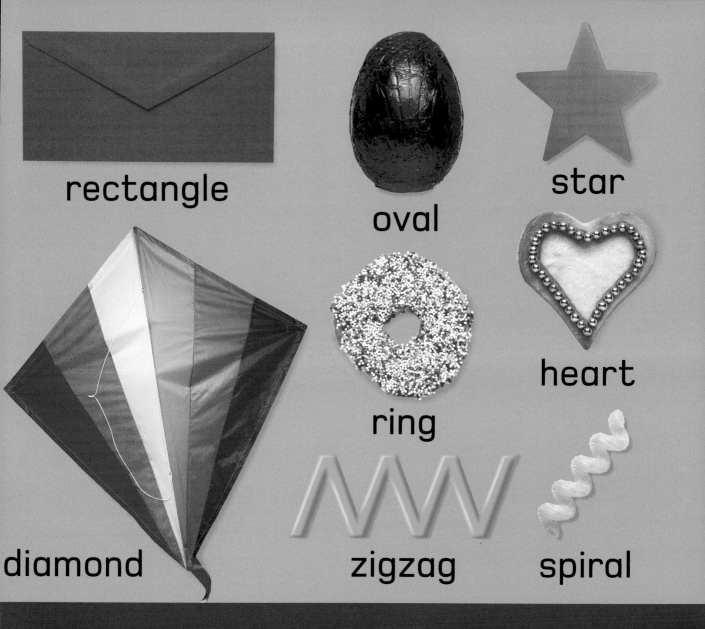

rectangle

oval

star

diamond

ring

heart

zigzag

spiral

What color is the star?

Numbers

one teddy bear two shoes three balls

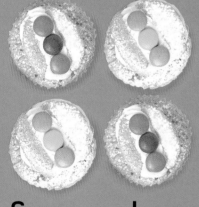

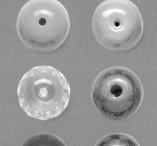

four cakes five toy cars six beads

What colors are the cars?

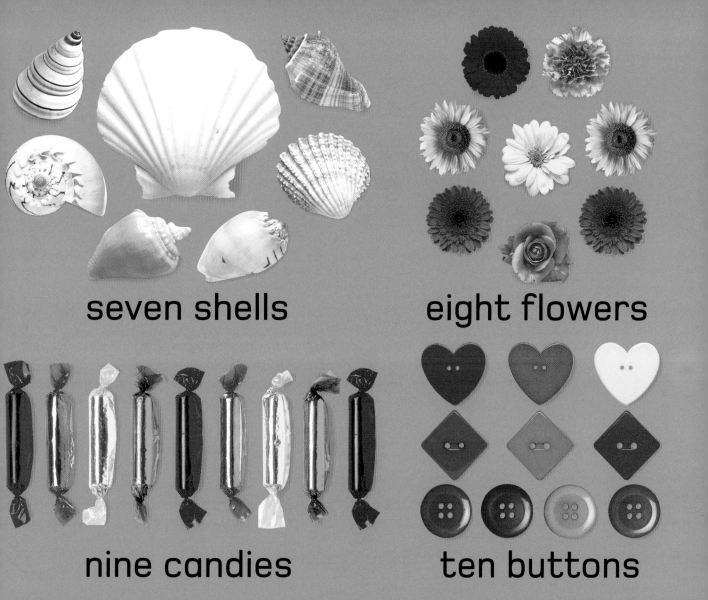

seven shells

eight flowers

nine candies

ten buttons

Which of these things can you eat?

What are they?

Can you name all of these things?